By Michael Anthony Steele

SCHOLASTIC INC.

New York   Toronto   London   Auckland   Sydney
Mexico City   New Delhi   Hong Kong   Buenos Aires

No part of this work may be reproduced in whole or in part, or stored in a retrieval system, or transmitted in any form or by any means, electronic, mechanical, photocopying, recording, or otherwise, without written permission of the publisher. For information regarding permission, write to Scholastic Inc., Attention: Permissions Department, 557 Broadway, New York, NY 10012.

ISBN 0-439-89719-X

© 2006 Eiichiro Oda / Shueisha, Toei Animation

Published by Scholastic Inc.
SCHOLASTIC and associated logos are trademarks and/or registered trademarks of Scholastic Inc.

12 11 10 9 8 7 6 5 4 3 2   6 7 8 9 10 11/0

Printed in the U.S.A.
First printing, October 2006

PROLOGUE

As Gold Roger was led from his cell, the harsh sunlight stung his eyes. He squinted through bangs of his greasy black hair. He could see hundreds of people gathered around gallows ahead. It seemed that everyone wanted to catch one last glimpse of the notorious pirate king. Gold Roger's thin mustache spread across his face as he grinned.

As he was led up the wooden steps, he couldn't help but chuckle. He had no regrets. By the end of his days, he had amassed wealth and power beyond anyone's wildest dreams. His name was known and feared far across the oceans. Even bound in chains, his guards dared not walk too close. Most pirates would go their entire lives without earning that mixture of fear and respect.

Once at the top platform, the guards moved him into position. They placed the noose around his neck and stepped back. A naval officer wearing a blue dress uniform climbed the platform steps. He unrolled a parchment scroll and stepped forward.

"Gold Roger," he said. "You are being charged with treason on the high seas, piracy, pillaging, robbery . . ."

"Forget the charges," growled the pirate. "Let's get on with this."

The officer sniffed and rolled up the paper. "Well then," he said. "Any final words?"

The pirate king stepped forward. He looked out at the hundreds of staring faces. "My fortune is yours for the taking," he boomed. He leaned back and bellowed with laughter. "But you'll have to find it first." He stopped laughing and stared into the crowd. "I left everything I own in *one piece*."

After Gold Roger's execution, a new age of

piracy was born. The seas teemed with outlandish ships and pirate captains who were just as eccentric. But, in spite of their differences, they all had one thing in common. Eventually, every pirate set sail for the mysterious Grand Line, searching for One Piece — the treasure that would make even the wildest dreams come true.

CHAPTER ONE

Shiro leaned against the wood railing and stared at the tiny island and let out a long sigh. He had become a sailor to find adventure and see the world. But all he saw was the same, boring sea. And, as it turned out, being a sailor on a luxury cruise ship was twice as boring. When the large schooner wasn't ferrying passengers, they were anchored off the coast of deserted islands throwing lavish parties. He knew they'd be there well into the night. Shiro sighed again. At least he had the tiny island to look at. Anything was better than looking at the endless sea.

"Check out that whirlpool," said a voice beside him. A young sailor named Tomeo leaned over the railing. He pointed to a swirling funnel in the water several yards away.

Shiro sighed. "Big deal." A whirlpool was hardly the adventure he craved.

THUNK! Something struck the side of the ship.

"What was that?" asked the younger sailor.

Shiro held on to his hat as he leaned over the railing. A small wooden barrel bobbed in the water beside the ship. "It's just a barrel."

Tomeo's eyes gleamed. "Let's pull it aboard."

Obviously the sailor was just as bored as Shiro. But the lad was right. Anything was better than staring over the railing for several more hours. He reached down and grabbed a hook and line. The long sturdy rope had a metal grappling hook tied to one end. He handed it to Tomeo.

The thin sailor swung it over his head in a circle. Shiro ducked as Tomeo let it fly toward the barrel. Unfortunately, the hook splashed into the ocean, a foot away from its target.

"That was so close," bragged Tomeo.

Shiro smirked. "In your dreams."

"Pipe down!" came a voice from the rigging above. "Can't a guy get some shut-eye?"

Shiro and Tomeo ignored the napping sailor. Instead, Shiro took a turn with the grappling hook. He swung it over his head and cast it toward the barrel. It hooked on to the soft wood on the first try.

The two sailors grunted as they pulled the barrel up the side of the ship.

"This is heavy," said Tomeo.

Shiro laughed. "I bet it's full of water." That would be just his luck. No adventure and nothing special inside the barrel.

They hauled it over the railing and dropped it to the deck. "It could be a barrel of monkeys," suggested Tomeo with a chuckle.

Shiro didn't answer. His eyes were on the dark ship sailing out from behind the nearby island. A sculpted goose's head and neck extended from its bow. Black hearts adorned its billowing sails. Then Shiro spotted something that chilled his blood. A black flag waved from the top of the ship's tallest mast. It bore the terrifying symbol of a skull and crossed bones. "Pirates off the port bow!" he yelled.

Tomeo released the barrel and ran to the railing. "They're moving their cannons into position." He pointed to the ship. "They're getting ready to attack!"

Shiro joined the rest of the sailors as they scrambled across the deck. This was not the kind of adventure he wanted. Now, he wished he could just stare at the calm and peaceful sea again.

CHAPTER TWO

Koby ran across the deck with an armful of swords. Hardened pirates pulled the cutlasses from his arms. After distributing the weapons, he ran to the ship's railing to join the rest of the pirates and their captain, Captain Alvida.

The self-proclaimed pirate queen was short but extremely wide. A long, thin grin spread across her face as her stringy black hair fluttered in the breeze. When her ship rounded on the luxury liner, she raised her huge spiked club into the air. "Fire!"

The cannons roared as lead balls sailed toward

their prey. Water exploded around the cruise ship. One of the shots smashed into the ship's mainmast. The tall wooden pole splintered and fell to the deck. It's mainsail draped over the fleeing crew.

As the pirate ship neared the helpless schooner, Captain Alvida turned to the young boy. "Ko-by!" she yelled.

Koby straightened his glasses and ran up to the large pirate. "Yes ma'am?"

She grimaced and leaned closer to him. "What?!"

Koby swallowed hard. "Yes, *Captain* ma'am!"

Alvida nodded and then held her head high. "Who's the loveliest one on the sea?"

Here we go again, Koby thought. He shuddered then forced a smile. "It's you, of course."

"Yes, it's true," she agreed. She flicked a strand of hair off her shoulder. "I'm gorgeous!" Her crew forced toothless grins and nodded in agreement.

Koby had never grown used to this disgusting ritual. Captain Alvida, who obviously *wasn't* the loveliest on the sea, was notorious for asking that question. When she wasn't barking orders or swiping her iron club at Koby or the men, she strode the deck of her pink ship, forcing compliments from the crew.

Her first mate, a muscular man with a thin mustache, pointed to the nearby ship. "What about the schooner, Captain?"

"Let's take 'em!" she roared. "And when Alvida takes you, you're taken for good!" The enormous woman howled with laughter.

The pirate crew scrambled to the railing as their ship pulled alongside the luxury liner. The men tossed grappling hooks toward the other ship's rigging. When their lines were set, they swung across to the crippled ship.

Koby flung a hook of his own. When it was firmly attached, he held tight with both hands. He tried to swing across but couldn't. Fear glued his feet to the wooden deck.

"Koby!" barked Alvida. "What are you doing?"

"I can't move," he replied. Sweat began to soak his white shirt. "I'm too afraid."

The hefty pirate stomped toward him. "Am I hearing things or did you dare talk back to me, you weasel?!"

Koby trembled. "Ahh! I'm sorry Miss Alvida Pirate ma'am."

Just then, Koby didn't have to worry about swinging over. Captain Alvida gave him a swift kick. "Get out of my face!" she ordered. Koby flew over the railing and tumbled across the deck of the other ship.

After Alvida leaped over, Koby tried to stay out of her way. He kept to the back of the crowd as the pirates stormed the ship's ballroom. The ship's well-dressed guests cowered at the other end of the large room.

Alvida's first mate laughed. "There's nothing to fear. We don't want your lives, just your valuables."

Alvida pushed through. "And we're talking cash, gold, and celebrity autographs!" She cackled with laughter.

Terrified, the guests gave in to the pirates' demands. The pirates moved through the crowd collecting wallets, purses, and jewelry.

Koby hated to see people treated so badly. He snuck out of the ballroom and climbed the stairs to the main deck. He decided to hide somewhere until the attack was over. He was almost free and clear when a large wooden barrel slammed into him.

Koby got to his feet and straightened his glasses. As he rolled the barrel out of the way, three of Alvida's pirates appeared behind him.

"You scurvy coward!" barked a broad pirate in a striped shirt. "You ought to walk the plank for not fighting with the rest of us!"

"T-t-t-that's not it . . ." Koby stammered. He looked down at the barrel. "I was, uh, thinking that maybe we could use some extra water."

A pirate with a tattoo on his face glanced at the barrel, then back at Koby. "Hmm, good idea."

"I agree with you, matey," said a pirate in the striped shirt. "Let's help." He picked up the barrel and set it on end.

Koby laughed nervously. "Heavy, right?"

"Can't be water inside," said the first pirate, scratching his head.

"Then what?" asked the tall, thin pirate.

"Time to find out." The big pirate made a fist. "A knuckle sandwich ought to do it."

Koby stepped back as the burly man raised his fist and reared back. Then, just as he was about to smash in the barrel, the top exploded. A young boy in a straw hat burst from the barrel like a giant jack-in-the-box. The boy stretched out his arms in a big yawn. One of his fists slammed into the large pirate's jaw. It sent him flying backwards. He collapsed onto the wooden deck, out cold.

The boy in the barrel was the strangest person Koby had ever seen.

CHAPTER THREE

Luffy yawned and stretched his arms wide. "That was a really great nap!" he said.

He didn't know how long he'd been asleep in the barrel. Just before his small boat went down in the whirlpool, Luffy had sealed himself inside the barrel in order to survive. He had then decided to take a nap as his barrel bobbed in the giant ocean. He knew he'd wake up after he was pulled aboard by the first passing ship. Luckily, all seemed to be going exactly as planned — that is, if Luffy ever made plans.

After his stretch, the boy took in his surroundings. He and his barrel stood on the deck of a large ship. A young boy with flaxen hair and thick glasses cowered in front of him. To his left, Luffy saw a large sailor in a striped shirt. The big man was stretched out on the deck, fast asleep.

Luffy laughed. "Strange place to fall asleep." He glanced down, seeing he still stood in his barrel. "Then again, I just took a nap in a barrel."

"Tell us your name!" shouted a voice behind him. "Or you'll be walking the plank to Davy Jones's locker!"

Luffy turned to see two snarling sailors. One had a tattoo across his face. The other was tall, thin, and wore a red bandana on his head. They both drew large swords and pointed them at Luffy.

"Who are you?" asked the tattooed man.

"Who cares?" asked the thin sailor. "Get him!"

The two sailors raised their swords and chopped down toward Luffy. When the blades hit the boy's shoulders, the swords snapped in two. Their sharp tips clattered across the deck.

Luffy chuckled. "You could hurt somebody, you know."

The pirates quivered as they stared at their broken swords. "Who are you?" asked the thin pirate.

Luffy held out a hand. "Monkey D. Luffy," he said. "But *Luffy* for short."

Neither sailor shook his hand. Instead, they grabbed the legs of the big napping man and dragged him away. Luffy shrugged and climbed out of the barrel. He straightened his maroon vest and casually tightened the fold of one of his rolled-up pant legs.

"Hey." The boy with the thick glasses tapped him on the shoulder. "You're in trouble."

"What do you mean?" asked Luffy.

"Captain Alvida!" the boy answered. "She's the pirate queen and she's going to get revenge on you!"

Luffy didn't know who this Alvida lady was. And, frankly, he didn't care. He had bigger problems. His stomach rumbled as he glanced around the ship. "So where do they keep the food?" He didn't wait for an answer. He strode to the nearest hatch.

The young boy followed him. "Are you out of

your mind, Luffy?" he asked. "Captain Alvida is horrible. Once she saw me drooling and made me swab the deck with my tongue!"

Luffy opened the hatch to see a large coil of rope. He slammed it shut and marched down the deck. "I need to find the storage room," said Luffy. "I'm hungry!"

Luffy opened another door and found exactly what he was searching for. "Wow! The food pantry! This is almost as good as finding buried treasure!" He bounded down the steps and looked over the goods. "What should I eat first? Let's see, there's cheese, bread, and apples!" Luffy opened a barrel of apples and grabbed one from the top. He took a big bite of the delicious fruit.

The young boy stood at the top of the stairs. "Luffy, my name is Koby."

"Glad to meet you, Koby," Luffy replied between bites.

Koby moved down the stairs and sat on the bottom step. "So tell me, what did you do to those pirates back there? That was amazing!"

"Crisp and sweet." Luffy finished off the apple

and grabbed another. "Is this a pirate ship?" he asked.

"No," answered Koby. "It's a passenger ship that's being raided by a pirate ship. And the name of the pirate captain is Alvida."

"Really?!" Luffy swallowed. "Are you a pirate, Koby? I mean, why else would you be hanging around a gang of pirates, right?"

"The truth is . . ." Koby hung his head. "I was supposed to be going on a fishing trip. Instead, I ended up on a boat running supplies to a pirate ship." He took off his glasses and wiped them on his shirt. "It was the scariest day of my life. It's been two years and I'm still alive because I do what they tell me to do."

Luffy finished off his second apple and ripped off a hunk of cheese from a cheese wheel. "Are you chicken or something?"

Koby glared at him. "Don't call me that!"

"Well, you could escape," Luffy suggested.

"No, I can't," said Koby. "If Captain Alvida caught me there's no telling what she would do. It's too dangerous."

Luffy finished his cheese. "So on top of being a chicken, you're stuck here for life?"

"You know, you're right, Luffy." Koby sighed. "I'm a coward. I don't even have the guts to hide in a barrel like you did. And yet, my dream is to be brave." He took off his glasses and wiped an eye. "So, how about you, Luffy?" he asked. "Is there something that you've always wanted to be?"

Luffy stood proudly. "Sure is! King of the Pirates!"

Koby almost dropped his glasses. "Ki-ki-king of the . . . Pirates?!"

"That's right," said Luffy.

"But why?" asked Koby.

Luffy chuckled. "Because that's what I want and that's that!"

"But pirates are cutthroats and treasure hunters and they don't follow orders. They're also smelly and have too much body hair!" He stood and marched over to Luffy. "Give me one good reason why you want to be King of the Pirates."

Luffy grinned. "One Piece."

"Impossible!" yelled Koby. "There's no way you'll ever find Gold Roger's treasure. Never!"

Luffy put a hand on the boy's shoulder. "Koby . . ."

Koby recoiled. "Don't hit me!" He crouched and covered his head.

"I wasn't going to hit you," said Luffy.

Koby slowly stood. "Oh, well, it wouldn't have been the first time. The pirates are always hitting me. I'm used to it."

"But that isn't right," said Luffy. "You should stick up for yourself." He stepped forward and put his hand back on the boy's shoulder. Koby jerked a bit, but didn't shrink away. "It's the same as sticking up for your dreams, Koby. You have to hang tough, no matter what."

Luffy finished off his hunk of cheese. "Well, now that I'm somewhat full, it's time to say good-bye." He patted Koby on the head. "Nice meeting you, Koby. Good luck with getting out of here."

Luffy strode up the stairs and reached for the door.

"Luffy?" said Koby. "Do you think I could join the navy?"

Luffy stopped and turned back to the young boy. "The navy?"

"Yes!" replied Koby. "It's always been my goal to uphold good over evil." His eyes sparkled. "My life's dream is to join the navy!" Then he looked down and wrung his hands. "Do you think I can do it?"

Luffy chuckled. "How would I know?"

Koby grimaced. "I'm tired of calling that pirate 'Captain ma'am' when she's just mean old Alvida."

"Koby!" shouted a woman's voice from the other side of the door.

Luffy leaped back just as the door exploded inward.

CHAPTER FOUR

Luffy and Koby were showered with splintered wood. As the dust settled, a large ugly woman stood on the other side of the broken doorway. A crowd of mean-looking pirates gathered behind her. Luffy recognized the two men he'd seen by the barrel.

The big woman pointed a huge spiked club at Koby. "Did I just hear you say that I'm old and mean?"

Koby held his arms over his head. "Please, don't hurt me!"

Alvida chuckled, then turned her attention to Luffy. "Is this that barrel monster you told me about?" The two pirates from before nodded. "Why, he ain't no monster." A grin stretched across her face. "He ain't even a bounty hunter like that pirate hunter, Zolo."

"Zolo?" asked Luffy.

"Koby!" The lady pirate slammed her club to the deck. "Tell this scurvy heathen who's the loveliest on the sea."

Koby shuffled forward. "Well, it's you of course, Miss Alvida Pirate ma'am."

Luffy's jaw dropped. "When was your last eye exam?"

The crowd of pirates gasped in unison. Alvida growled as veins rose on her forehead.

"What?!!" Alvida barked. She charged into the room and swung her club at Luffy. He leaped out of the way as it slammed against the crate full of apples.

Luffy landed by Koby and grabbed his arm. "Let's go," he said as he dragged Koby past the huge woman. They zipped by the other pirates and ran out onto the open deck.

Koby slipped from Luffy's grip and darted toward the ship's railing. Luffy found himself surrounded by angry pirates. Each of them had their swords drawn and ready. Luffy ducked as one sword sliced toward his head. He leaned to the side as another pirate attacked from above. When the pirate's head was close, Luffy slammed his own head into the pirate's. The brute crumpled to the deck.

Luffy flipped backwards as the rest of the mob chopped at him. He landed on his feet just as another pirate charged. Luffy sidestepped his attacker and grabbed him by the arm. "Thanks for dropping by," he taunted. "But now it's time to go!" Luffy threw the pirate against the others. They tumbled like a set of bowling pins.

Luffy chuckled and straightened his hat. However, as he turned to leave, he saw the rest of Alvida's crew standing behind him. The angry horde snarled as they raised their sharp swords.

"I can't fight all of you!" said Luffy. He turned

and ran down the open deck. The mob of pirates yelled as they chased him.

"Get him!" one cried.

"Throw him to the sharks!" shouted another.

As Luffy ran, he reached out and grabbed the ship's mainmast. With his fingers firmly gripping the wooden pole, he kept running toward the ship's bow. His arm stretched several yards behind him. He looked over his shoulder to see the pirates had stopped and were staring at his elongated arm.

When Luffy reached the front of the ship, he stopped and laughed. "Fooled you!" Luffy took a few more steps forward, stretching his arm a bit farther. "Gum Gum Rocket!" He jumped off the ground as his elastic arm yanked him toward the pirates. They dropped their swords and ran but it was too late. Gaining speed, Luffy slammed into the crowd, sending them flying across the ship. Luffy tumbled to a stop. He stood up among a ship's deck littered with moaning pirates.

Koby ran up to him. "Luffy, who or what in the world are you?" he asked.

"Oh yeah," said Luffy. He hooked a finger into

the side of his mouth and pulled it outward. The side of his face stretched a foot away from his head. "I'm a rubber man."

Koby pointed at him. "You ate the Cursed Fruit?"

CHAPTER FIVE

Koby couldn't believe his eyes. Not only did Luffy pop out of a barrel and have the courage to stand up to Alvida and her pirates, he had also eaten the Cursed Fruit.

Everyone who's ever sailed knew the legend of the Cursed Fruit. If you take one bite, you'll gain powers no one has ever known. Some give you the power to spit fire, others the power to create tidal waves, or even the power to turn into rubber like Luffy. There was a different Cursed Fruit for each one of these special powers. However, those powers came with a hefty price for anyone who loved the sea. Anyone who ate the fruit would no longer be able to swim.

Alvida stomped toward them. "Well, what do you know. That pirate legend about the Cursed Fruit is really true!"

"It sure is," said Luffy. He let go of the corner of his mouth. His face snapped back into place. "And guess what?" He jutted a thumb toward his chest. "I'm a pirate just like you!"

"So, you're a pirate. Do you know what that means?" Alvida tapped her heavy club in one hand. "It means that you're the competition, rubber boy."

Koby shuffled over to Luffy and tugged on his vest. "Let's scram."

"How come?" asked Luffy. The boy looked as if he really didn't know what kind of danger Alvida posed to them.

Koby pointed to the evil woman. "You see her club, don't you? Well, she sure knows how to use it."

Koby was amazed. Luffy didn't seem frightened at all. The boy had laughed as he took on Alvida's entire crew. Now, the meanest and ugliest pirate that

Koby had ever known loomed over them and Luffy didn't seem to care.

"Koby," said Alvida in her sickeningly sultry voice. "Who's the loveliest on the sea?"

Koby couldn't take it anymore. Luffy was brave enough to follow his dreams; why couldn't Koby do the same? Luffy's words echoed in his head. *Because that's what I want and that's that!*

Koby trembled with anger. He balled up his fists and glared at the humungous woman. "Not you, you ugly old bag!"

Luffy leaned back and howled with laughter.

Alvida's eyes widened. "You're going to pay for that, Koby!"

"Oh, yeah?" said Koby. He couldn't stop himself. It was as if his mouth had a mind of its own. "Well, if you have trouble finding me, try looking on a navel ship because that's where I'll be!"

Alvida's eye twitched as the veins in her forehead throbbed. "Have you lost your mind, you little weasel?"

"Maybe so, but at least I found my courage," barked Koby. "You can't bully me anymore! And once

I join the navy, I'll hunt you down and throw you in irons!"

Alvida raised her spiked club over her head. "That's enough!"

Koby ignored the instinct to run and cower. He wasn't going to wimp out this time. He had finally stood up for himself and his dream.

"Way to go!" said Luffy. The odd boy jumped in front of Koby just as the pirate's club flew toward them. The club slammed onto his head, but Luffy didn't move. He smiled and cut an eye toward Alvida. "Is that it?"

"What?" asked Alvida. For the first time in two years, Koby saw fear in the fat pirate's eyes.

Luffy jerked his head upward, knocking the club from Alvida's hand. "That's what!"

Alvida shook with fear as Luffy made a fist and pulled back one arm. Koby couldn't believe it as he watched Luffy's arm stretch back off the ship and over the sea. It looked as if his arm stretched back a full mile.

"Gum Gum Blast!" Luffy's arm retracted with enormous speed. It flew back to the ship and slammed into Alvida's big belly. The pirate yelled as Luffy's fist sent her flying off the ship and over the horizon.

"Wow!" said Koby.

Luffy retracted his arm and marched toward the ship's railing. He pointed to the three pirates still aboard Alvida's nearby ship. They trembled at the sight of him.

"You there!" said Luffy. "Launch a boat for Koby on the double! He's joining the navy." He smiled. "Unless any of you object."

"No, sir!" yelped one of the pirates. "I mean, yes, sir!" They scrambled over each other trying to get to the nearby life boat.

Koby joined Luffy at the rail. "Thank you!" he said.

Luffy opened his mouth to answer. Then cannonballs slammed into the water beside them.

CHAPTER SIX

What now? Luffy thought.

Three plumes of water exploded around the two ships. Luffy stumbled as the deck rocked with the nearby explosions. High-pitched whistles sounded as more cannonballs sailed toward them.

Luffy turned around and saw three large naval ships approaching them. "There's your navy, Koby." Their large sails billowed in the wind. "Timing's everything and now's your time to enlist."

"What?" asked Koby.

"And now's my time to scram," said Luffy. He leaped over the railing and landed in the small sailboat being lowered by the pirates.

He wasn't the only one with thoughts of escaping. Alvida's dazed crew stumbled to their feet and scrambled back to their ship.

"Hold on!" yelled Koby. He jumped in after him. "They'll never let me enlist this way. They'll think I'm a pirate and throw me in jail."

Once the boys were aboard, the pirates let go of the ropes. Luffy and Koby held tight as the boat dropped to the water below.

As they splashed down, another cannonball struck the water beside them. Luffy and Koby got busy with the boat's rigging. Luffy unfurled the boat's only sail while Koby grabbed the rudder. Soon their bow pointed toward the open sea. The naval ships and the pirates were behind them. The ships were so busy fighting, no one noticed their escape.

For a long time, neither boy said a word. Koby tended the rudder while Luffy sat on the ship's bow. The cool, salty breeze felt good blowing against Luffy's face.

"I don't know how we did it," said Koby, breaking the silence. "We're lucky we escaped."

"Yeah," agreed Luffy. "It sure was fun!"

"Luffy, I have one question," said Koby.

"What's that?" asked Luffy.

"You know, if you search for One Piece, it means sailing a ship to the Grand Line, right?" asked Koby.

"That's right," replied Luffy.

"But Luffy, do you know how dangerous it's supposed to be?" asked Koby.

Koby was right. The Grand Line was a long, thin continent that separated the great oceans. Few pirates ever saw it. And it's said that those who did, never returned.

"That's why I'll need a good pirate crew." Luffy hopped off the ship's bow and walked back to Koby. "Alvida said something about a pirate hunter. What was his name again?"

"You mean Zolo?" asked Koby. "But he's a pirate *hunter*, not a pirate. There's a big difference."

Luffy laughed. "Not really, as long as he's a nice guy."

Koby's eyes widened. "But he isn't! He's an awful man. A vicious monster! Besides, I hear he's under arrest."

Luffy tightened a knot on the rigging. "Hey, if this Zolo turns out to be a nice person, then I'll just help him escape."

Luffy climbed back to the ship's bow. He smiled as they sailed toward the setting sun.

"You think you can make anything happen, don't you?" asked Koby.

"Sure do," replied Luffy.

CHAPTER SEVEN

The next morning, a small dot appeared on the horizon. As the sun slowly brightened the sky, the dot grew larger. Soon, Luffy and Koby's destination came into perfect view. It was Naval Base Island. The large island jutted out of the sea like a large rock in the middle of a flat sandy desert. Trees, shops, and houses covered its rim while the tall naval base pushed out of its center. At the middle of the base stood a tall tower painted with blue and gray camouflage. Luffy had never been to Naval Base Island. He couldn't wait to see what adventures waited for him there.

As they neared the docks at the edge of the island, Luffy rolled up the sail. As Koby steered them in, Luffy grabbed a line and prepared to hop out of the boat.

"Luffy, are you sure sailing to a naval base is such a good idea?" asked Koby.

Luffy leaped off the boat and onto the wooden dock. "You worry too much," he said. He pulled the rope and eased the boat closer to the small pier.

"This is no laughing matter," Koby warned. "The navy hates pirates. And you're a pirate!"

Luffy tied off the ship. "I'm going to be king!" He marched up the pier toward a set of steps leading to the city above.

"You're not listening!" Koby scrambled out of the boat and ran to catch up. "The navy's only half your trouble. The man you're after is Roronoa Zolo. And he doesn't just hunt down pirates. They say he slices them up and feeds them to the fishes!"

Luffy wasn't really listening. He topped the stairs and looked at the city before him. Several wooden shops and houses lined narrow streets. The island teemed with life. Sailors and shopkeepers alike roamed the streets, darting in and out of shops, and admiring the wares of street venders.

Excited, Luffy cupped his hands around his mouth. "Hello!" he shouted. "Hey, Naval Base Island, here I am!" A few people stopped and looked his way. Then they quickly returned to what they were doing. Luffy marched toward town.

"Luffy, be reasonable," said Koby. The young boy ran after him. "Even if you bust Zolo out of the brig, there's no way he's going to join your pirate crew."

"Relax, Koby," said Luffy. He zeroed in on a fruit vendor. "I'm only going to ask him to join me."

"Have you lost your mind?" asked Koby. "He *hunts* pirates like you!"

Luffy didn't answer. Instead, he grabbed a fresh pear from an open crate. "Ooh, these look good." Luffy wiped it on his vest and took a bite. It was delicious. He reached into his pant pocket and dug out a coin. He tossed it to the woman running the stand.

Luffy looked around. "I wonder where they're keeping Zolo."

Suddenly, all the shopkeepers and patrons gasped. They turned and stared at Luffy with wide eyes. A few even ducked behind barrels and crates.

Koby leaned close to Luffy. "Do you think they'd be so afraid if Zolo was a nice guy?" he whispered.

Luffy shook his head and chuckled. He took another bite of the pear as he continued down the street. Koby walked alongside him.

They turned a corner then proceeded down a street heading toward the center of the island. Then Luffy had an idea. "Hey, while I look for Zolo at the base you can enlist in the navy."

Koby lowered his head. "I don't know if I'm ready. As soon as I feel more confident . . . that's when I'll go see Captain Morgan."

Just as before, an entirely new crowd of shopkeepers and customers gasped in unison. Some ran away while others ducked into nearby shops.

Luffy leaned back and laughed. "This town cracks me up!"

Koby glanced around nervously. "I think this whole town is cracking up. How can they be as afraid of Captain Morgan as they are of that cut-throat, Zolo?"

After a few more twists and turns, Luffy and Koby made their way to the base at the center of the island. A tall stone wall surrounded the giant tower. Two thick iron gates marked the base's entrance.

"This must be the place," said Luffy. "It looks so big."

Koby sighed. "Yeah, and I guess this means good-bye, Luffy. I'm going to miss you."

Luffy didn't hear him. Instead, he walked away from the giant gates. He found a low part of the stone wall and jumped up. He grabbed the top with his hands and pulled himself to the top. "Hey, Koby," he shouted. "Come here and check this out."

Koby ran to the bottom of the wall. "You're trespassing! Get down!"

Luffy scanned the open field in front of him. "Well, don't see any pirate hunters," he said.

"Of course not," said Koby. He struggled to climb up and join Luffy. "Zolo's probably in their deepest, darkest dungeon."

Luffy pointed to the only thing in the open

area. "There's just that guy." A thin man was tied to a post in the center of the yard. He slouched against his bonds and drooped his head forward.

"Hey, you're right," said Koby. "There's that guy wearing a black bandana, a green waistband . . ." Koby gasped. "Wait a minute! I've never seen him, but I've heard all the stories!" Koby nearly fell off the wall. "That's Zolo!"

"Great," said Luffy. "All I have to do is untie those ropes and he's free."

"Free to filet you like fresh fish," whispered Koby. "This guy is a monster! He eats pirates like you for breakfast!"

"Hey," said the man in the courtyard. "You two . . ." His voice was low and raspy.

Koby's eyes widened. "He's talking to us."

"Get out of here!" Zolo ordered.

"Let's do what he says!" said Koby.

"I mean now!" Zolo barked.

Koby tugged on Luffy's vest. "I'm begging you, Luffy. Please don't set that horrible hunter free! It'll be the end of us!"

CHAPTER EIGHT

Luffy didn't care what Koby said. He had to talk to Zolo and find out what kind of guy he was. He was just about to throw a leg over the wall when the end of a ladder appeared beside him. A young girl climbed the ladder and hopped over the fence. When she hit the ground, she looked back at the boys and put a finger to her mouth. "Shh!"

"What's she doing?" asked Koby. "Luffy, stop her. She'll be torn to shreds by that beast."

The little girl scampered over to Zolo. Her short brown hair bobbed as she ran. When she reached the bound man, she dug into a pocket in her dress. "I figured you must be hungry," she said. "So I baked you some cookies."

"Stop bugging me, little girl!" Zolo growled. "Get lost!"

The girl wasn't frightened at all. "Don't they look good?" she asked. "I made them all by myself." She giggled. "And I only dropped in one eggshell."

Zolo struggled against his ropes. "I don't need anything from a sea urchin like you. Now get out of here."

"But I thought . . ."

"Get out while you still can!" Zolo yelled.

Just then, something rattled at the other end of the compound. Luffy saw a metal gate slide open and a group of men walk through. A wiry man strode toward Zolo and the girl. The man had short blond hair and wore a fancy blue suit. Two sailors walked behind him. The men wore white naval uniforms with black scarves. Their naval caps were pulled down to just above their eyes.

"Zolo, Zolo, Zolo," said the man in a shrill voice. "Where are your manners?" The girl trembled as the strange man approached. He pointed to her. "Is that any way to talk to a child? I'll tell my father on you. Truly I will."

"Who's that guy that's dressed like a weirdo?" whispered Luffy.

"He's navy," Koby replied. "Which means that little girl will be all right."

The man leaned over and snatched a cookie from the girl's hands. "Aah! Yummy! Don't mind if I do."

"Leave her alone, Helmeppo!" ordered Zolo.

"Hey! That's not for you!" protested the girl.

The man called Helmeppo popped the cookie into his mouth. After a couple of chews, he gagged with disgust. "Horrible!" He spit cookie crumbs to the ground. "What did you put in there? Barnacles? Rotting fish heads?"

"No, sir. I put in a cup of sugar and . . ." said the little girl.

Helmeppo didn't let her finish. He slapped the other two cookies from her hand. Then he stomped them into the ground.

"Stop it!" yelled the girl. "Stop!"

"Oh, man," said Koby. "I can't believe they'd let such a mean guy in the navy."

"There!" Helmeppo chuckled. "Now they look as bad as they taste."

Tears welled in the girl's eyes. "But I worked so hard on them."

"Pity," said Helmeppo. "But didn't you know that helping a criminal is a criminal offense?" He brushed back one of his blond locks. "So says my father, Captain Morgan."

"Father?" whispered Luffy.

"He's the son of Captain Morgan?" asked Koby.

Helmeppo pointed to one of the sailors. "Throw her over the fence!" The man hesitated. "You better do as you're told or I'll report you to my father."

The sailor snapped to attention. "Yes, sir!" Then he bent down and picked up the girl. "I'm really sorry," he told her.

Luffy couldn't believe his eyes. The sailor carried her to the wall and threw her as hard as he could. She flew high into the air.

CHAPTER NINE

Luffy didn't think. He leaped up after the flying girl. Unfortunately, he was too far away to catch her. That would have been a problem for any normal boy. Fortunately, it wasn't a problem for someone who had eaten the Cursed Fruit. Luffy stretched out his arms. They reached out five times the length of his body. His hands caught the girl and his body snapped toward her like a rubber band. He held her tightly as he safely bounced to the ground.

He let go and the girl got to her feet. "You saved my life!" she said.

Koby ran up to them. "Awesome catch, Luffy. Way to go!" He put a hand on the girl's shoulder. "Are you okay? I can't believe the navy is acting like this. It doesn't make sense."

"Bilge rat!" yelled Zolo from behind the wall.

The three kids ran back and peeked over the edge.

Helmeppo sneered. "A man in your position really ought to watch his tongue."

"Say what you want," said Zolo. "But I'll survive the month, no problem. Just ten more days!"

"We shall see," said Helmeppo. He turned and strode out of the courtyard. The two sailors followed. "Your sentence isn't over yet, Zero, I mean Zolo."

When the men were gone, Luffy hopped over the fence. He had to get a closer look at the pirate hunter.

Zolo raised his head and glared at Luffy. "What are you still doing here? I thought I told you minnows to swim away before you become shark bait!"

"They say you're a bad guy," said Luffy. "But I want to know if you're strong."

"That's none of your business," said Zolo. "Now get lost."

Luffy turned to leave. "Well, if you don't want help."

"Not so fast!" Zolo growled. "See that?" He nodded toward the smashed cookie. "Get it for me."

Luffy knelt by the small pile of cookie crumbs. "What are you going to do with this thing?" He scooped up what he could. "It's full of sand and mud."

"I'm going to eat it," Zolo sneered. "Why? Because I'm a survivor!"

Luffy shrugged and tossed it toward the bound man. Zolo snatched it up in one bite. He choked a bit as he chewed.

"Tough to swallow?" asked Luffy.

Zolo coughed and gulped it down his throat. "No, it was good." He looked Luffy in the eye. "Tell her thank you."

Luffy ran back to the wall and hopped over. He and Koby walked the little girl back to town. As they traveled, the boys learned that her name was Rika. Her mother owned a local restaurant.

"So, you think he really liked my cookies?" asked Rika.

"Sure do," replied Luffy. "He said to give his compliments to the chef."

Rika beamed. "I'm glad!"

"Maybe Zolo isn't so bad after all," said Koby. "Still, everyone says he's a beast."

"Not true," said Rika. "You see, Zolo went to prison to save me and my mother."

"Save you?" asked Luffy. "What are you talking about?"

"It's all because of that mean man," explained Rika. "Helmeppo, the evil son of Captain Morgan!"

Rika told them how, one day, Helmeppo was out terrorizing the town with his vicious pet wolf. It was during lunch and her mother had just finished serving some customers. Rika was busy sweeping up when Helmeppo's wolf barged in. The giant beast put his front paws on the nearest table and began eating from a customer's plate.

Helmeppo strolled in like he owned the place. "Make room," he ordered. "My sweet pet is hungry." He sat down at a table as two of his sailors stood behind him. Helmeppo never went anywhere without two of his men to protect him.

Rika didn't think. She swatted the wolf with the end of her broom. "Get out, you flea bag!"

Both the wolf and Helmeppo snarled at her. "You shouldn't have done that," said Helmeppo. "The sentence for striking my pet is a month in prison!"

"She didn't mean it!" cried her mother. "Tell him you're sorry, honey!"

The wolf growled and leaped toward her. Just as its powerful jaws were almost upon her, a stool slammed into the wolf, knocking it across the room. The wolf was out cold.

"Who did that?" asked Helmeppo.

Rika looked around. She wondered who saved her as well. The rest of the customers were huddled against the wall. All of them but one. A man wearing a black bandana and green waistband sat at the bar, eating lunch.

"You're that pirate hunter, Zolo!" said Helmeppo.

Zolo didn't look up from his meal. "Don't bother me, I'm eating."

Helmeppo's face flushed. "I'm Captain Morgan's son. How dare you challenge me?!" He pulled his sword from his belt and waved it at the pirate hunter.

"You're not serious, are you?" asked Zolo.

Helmeppo yelled and charged him. He chopped at Zolo with his thick cutlass. The pirate hunter pushed away from the bar as the blade passed inches from his face. He leaped from the stool and kicked the sword from Helmeppo's hand. The sharp cutlass stuck into the ceiling above. Then Zolo spun around and slammed a foot into the man's chest. Helmeppo flew against the bar and crumpled to the floor.

"You have no idea what trouble you're in," said Helmeppo. He began to get to his feet. The two sailors stepped forward.

Zolo produced a samurai sword and the sailors froze. "Really?" He pulled the sword from its sheath and pointed it at Helmeppo. "From where I stand, you've got it backwards."

"Don't be hasty," Helmeppo growled. "Touch just one hair and everyone in this tavern will hang from the highest gallows for treason, including women and children." He glared up at the pirate hunter. "My father, Captain Morgan, will see to that!" The captain's son slowly got to his feet. Zolo kept his blade pointed at him as he rose. "But I'll make you a deal," said Helmeppo. "I won't send the child and her mother to prison if you go in their place. For one month."

"One month?" asked Zolo. He dropped his sword to the floor. "Piece of cake."

Rika led Luffy and Koby into her mother's restaurant. The boys met her mother and she gave them as much food as they could eat for helping her daughter. Rika finished her story while they finished their lunch.

"Zolo's only been tied up there for three weeks so far," Rika explained. "I don't think he can last a whole month." A tear ran down her cheek. "It's all my fault."

"You shouldn't blame yourself," said Koby.

If Luffy hadn't seen Helmeppo for himself, he'd have a hard time believing anyone could be so rotten. One thing was for certain, this Zolo seemed like just the kind of person he needed on his crew.

Suddenly, the restaurant doors slammed open. "I'm back," yelled Helmeppo. He marched into the room and plopped down at one of the tables. As always, his two sailors stood on either side of him. "Remember me?" He leaned back in the chair and propped his feet on the table. "I think you owe me a free meal for all the trouble you caused me last time. Don't you agree?"

Rika's mother didn't say a word. She nervously brought him a plate of crabs' legs. As Helmeppo cracked one open, an evil grin spread across his face. "And bring me a bottle of your finest juice," he added.

Luffy looked around the restaurant. All of the customers looked away from the obnoxious man. It's as if they were too afraid he'd notice them and punish them for merely looking into his eyes. Luffy couldn't believe anyone so foolish could be so feared.

"Oh, and I almost forgot," Helmeppo said between bites. "I've decided to execute that Zolo tomorrow. It's been so dull around here and I need a good laugh."

That was all Luffy could take. Someone had to teach this maniac a lesson. He ran across the room and punched Helmeppo in the face. The blond man flew out of his chair and tumbled to the floor.

Helmeppo grabbed his jaw as the sailors helped him to his feet. "Are you crazy?" he asked.

Luffy wanted to give him a second helping but Koby grabbed him from behind. "Luffy, stop!" Koby ordered. "That's enough!"

Luffy glared at the captain's son. "You're a coward!" he yelled.

"You hit me?" asked Helmeppo. "But I'm the son of Captain Morgan!"

Luffy struggled to break free. "I don't care whose son you are!"

"When I tell father, you're history," Helmeppo warned.

"Please calm down," said Koby. "There's no sense getting the navy against you like Zolo."

"I don't care," Luffy told him.

CHAPTER TEN

Captain Morgan sat at his desk and stared out the window. From the top of the tall naval tower, he couldn't see much of the island below. His view consisted mostly of the ocean. That's just the way he liked it. He often thought of the tiny island as his ship and every resident was part of his crew. To rule a crew, a captain needed an iron fist. Captain Morgan had something better than that. He had a giant battle axe instead of a right hand. That is why the name "Axe-Hand" Morgan was feared throughout the island.

He turned his thoughts back to the lone sailor

shivering in the center of his huge office. However, Morgan kept his back to him and continued to stare at the sea. "Sailor, am I not the greatest captain this island has ever known?" he asked.

"Yes, sir. Captain Morgan, sir," barked the sailor.

The captain stroked his steel jaw with his left hand. "Then why haven't the people delivered my weekly bribe?"

"Well, sir," the sailor's voice cracked. "They said they gave you every piece of gold last week, sir."

Morgan spun around. "Greedy liars!" he roared. "Go and search their homes!"

The sailor saluted. "Yes, sir, Captain Morgan, sir!" He turned and sprinted for the door.

Helmeppo pushed the sailor aside as he darted into the room. "Father!" he yelled. "There's a boy in town who punched me in the face. You must hang him!"

The captain rolled his eyes as he got to his feet. He had more important things to deal with than the problems of his sniveling son. He marched toward the door, handling Helmeppo the way he always handled him. He ignored him.

Morgan stomped up the stairs toward the roof. His son followed but luckily he kept his mouth shut. The captain squinted as he emerged into the sunlight. The rooftop was bustling with activity. He'd had all the sailors under his command working on a project of the utmost importance — erecting a giant statue of himself. The enormous sculpture was the perfect likeness. The statue would stand atop the base, arms outstretched, master of all it surveyed. A hundred sailors tugged on ropes, positioning the statue before it was raised.

"Careful, swabbies," Morgan warned. "If anyone so much as chips this, he'll walk the plank!" He slowly paced around the giant sculpture.

Helmeppo was close behind. "Father!" he yelled. "I *order* you to take revenge on the scoundrel who struck me!"

Morgan stopped in his tracks. He slowly turned and glared down at his worthless son.

Helmeppo started to shake. "It was outrageous."

He laughed nervously. "No one's ever done that. Not even you."

Morgan stomped toward him. "And do you know why I've never beaten you?"

Helmeppo smiled. "Because you love me?"

"Don't be ridiculous!" yelled the captain. He struck Helmeppo with the back of his hand. His son flew across the roof, and the captain stomped after him. "The reason I never beat you until today is because you're just too stupid! It wasn't worth the trouble!" Morgan reached his axe hand toward Helmeppo and hooked it into his jacket. "But today you gave me an order. And *nobody* gives Captain Morgan orders!" The captain lifted his son off the ground and brought him closer to his face. "Do you understand, sonny boy?"

"Yes, father," said Helmeppo.

The captain turned his axe over, dropping his son. Helmeppo fell in a heap onto the roof. "Is it true someone tried to help one of our prisoners today?" asked the captain.

"Yes," replied Helmeppo. "And I punished that little girl promptly."

The captain stroked his steel jaw. "Did you execute her?"

"What?" asked his son. "No! She was just a little girl."

The captain turned to one of his commanders. The older man snapped to attention. "Go into the town," ordered the captain. "Find this traitor and put an end to her!"

The commander's eyes widened. "But, sir, she's just a child."

Captain Morgan couldn't believe his ears. "No one disobeys my orders!" he yelled. "Not a child and not a sailor! Now go and put an end to her!"

The commander didn't budge. "Sir, I can't . . ."

"Can't?!!" roared the captain. He swatted the commander with the flat side of his axe. "Throw him in the dungeon!" the captain ordered. Several sailors grabbed the commander and dragged him away.

"A leader must rule with an iron fist," said Morgan. "Anyone disagree?"

"No, sir!" barked the sailors in unison. "You're right, sir!"

The captain patted his axe. "I will take care of

the girl personally, but first we must attend to more important business." He pointed to the statue. "Be careful as you raise this glorious masterpiece!"

The sailors scrambled back to their ropes. They each heaved and the sculpture slowly rose into place.

"Look at it, men!" Morgan spread his arms wide, mimicking the statue. "The magnificent symbol of my power!" The captain turned toward the sea. "Let the world marvel at my greatness!"

CHAPTER ELEVEN

Luffy hopped the stone fence and traipsed over to the bound pirate hunter. Sweat dripped from Zolo's brow as he raised his head. "Well, well, look what the tide washed in," he said.

Luffy stopped and crossed his arms. "If I untie your ropes, then you have to be part of my crew."

Zolo shook his head. "I must be hallucinating."

"No, really," said Luffy. "I want you in my pirate crew! You can even be my first mate!"

"Pirate?" asked Zolo. "In case you haven't heard I'm a pirate *hunter*! Which means no deal!"

"Hey, what do you have against pirates?" asked Luffy.

"You can't trust them," replied Zolo. "They're a bunch of money-grubbing thieves."

Luffy laughed. "That's the pot calling the kettle black. You're the mercenary. You hunt pirates for money." He pushed back his straw hat. "I do it for the adventure!"

"I'm a sword fighter, not a mercenary," said Zolo. "And there isn't a thing I've done that I regret." He looked Luffy in the eyes. "I'll survive no matter what. I don't need to join a crew to accomplish my goals."

Luffy laughed. "But I've already made up my mind. You're joining my crew."

Zolo smirked. "Don't count on it."

Luffy looked around. "Hey, doesn't a sword fighter need his sword?" Zolo didn't answer. "Well, if you promise to join my crew," said Luffy, "then the first thing I'll do is go and find your legendary sword."

"Is this some kind of bribe?" asked Zolo.

"Yup," Luffy replied.

"Well, at least you're honest enough to admit it," said Zolo.

Luffy grabbed Zolo's post and began to step backwards. His arm stretched out before him.

"Hey! Have your brains turned to jellyfish?" asked Zolo. "What are you doing?"

"Gum Gum Rocket!" said Luffy. He hopped off the ground and his arm jerked him forward. He soared out of the field and over the metal gate.

Luffy flew toward the base of the tall tower. He hit the ground and rolled to a stop. He expected to land smack in the middle of patrolling sailors and naval officers. He was all ready for a fight. However, there was no one around.

"Where'd everybody go?" asked Luffy. "This is really strange."

"Pull it up!" shouted a distant voice.

Luffy peered up at the top of the tower. He heard several grunts and the creaking of ropes. Something was happening up there. Luffy shot a hand toward the sky. His arm stretched and stretched longer and longer. When it reached the top of the tower, his hand grabbed the edge and held tight.

"And away we go!" said Luffy. "Gum Gum Rocket!"

Luffy hopped up and his arm pulled him toward the top of the tower. As he reached the top, his arm snapped back into shape. Unfortunately, Luffy kept flying upward. "A little too much rocket!"

Luckily, a huge statue leaned at the top of the tower. It had several ropes dangling from its top. Luffy grabbed one of the ropes to stop himself from shooting over the island. The line pulled taught and the boy swung back around the roof.

Just then, he noticed that several sailors stood on the roof holding ropes of their own. They all pulled at a giant statue of a man with an axe for a hand. Then Luffy realized he was swinging in the opposite direction. Several of the sailors were thrown off balance and the statue began to fall. The men had no choice but to release their lines. The giant sculpture smashed to the roof with a loud *CRACK!* The top half of the statue snapped off and tumbled over the edge. It smashed to the ground.

"No!!" yelled a large man. He towered over the rest of the sailors. He wore a long blue coat, had a jagged steel jaw, and a huge battle axe on one hand. Luffy thought he must be Captain Morgan.

"That was careless of me," Luffy told him. "Sorry."

The captain pointed at Luffy. "This is treason!" he roared. "Get him!"

Then Luffy spotted Helmeppo. The coward pointed toward Luffy as well. "Father! He's the one who hit me. I told you he was trouble!"

Luffy didn't wait for the men to follow the captain's orders. He stretched out an arm and wrapped it around Helmeppo. He snatched him off the ground and hauled him toward the rooftop door. "I've been looking for you," Luffy told him. "I need you to help me find something."

"Father, save me!" cried Helmeppo.

Luffy dragged the captain's son down the stairs and through a hallway. He heard the captain's men close behind him. Although Helmeppo struggled, Luffy easily pulled him along as he ducked into another hallway and down another set of stairs. The cowardly man bumped down the steps behind him.

As Luffy darted through the new corridor, he

looked down at his prisoner. "Tell me where you stashed Zolo's sword!" he ordered.

Helmeppo waved his hand. "Stop!" He pointed back down the hallway. "In my room. You passed it."

"Why didn't you say so before?" Luffy asked. "Now I have to drag you all the way back."

Luffy turned and saw four sailors blocking his path. "Let him go!" one of them ordered. They each aimed a rifle at Luffy. "Or we'll be forced to shoot you!"

CHAPTER TWELVE

Captain Morgan leaned over the roof's edge and stared at what was left of his statue. All that time and money lay crumbled before him. It would take at least a month's bribes from the townspeople for him to build another one.

The captain fumed as he thought of the strange boy kidnapping his son. He would destroy that whelp if it was the last thing he did. Not because he had kidnapped Helmeppo. Morgan could not care less about his good-for-nothing son. The boy's attack on the statue was just as bad as attacking the captain himself.

When Morgan had given the order, the surrounding sailors dropped their ropes and ran through the roof's exit. However, one sailor remained. He looked over the edge of the rooftop. The captain raised his axe. He wouldn't have any more disobedience today.

"Sir, look!" shouted the man. He pointed downward. "On the field of dishonor. Someone's trespassing and they're heading for the prisoner!"

"What?" asked Morgan. He spotted another boy scampering toward the bound pirate hunter. He wore a white shirt and eyeglasses. Captain Morgan roared. "I'm surrounded by traitors!"

The captain stomped toward the rooftop door. He'd let his men capture Helmeppo's kidnapper. Morgan planned to take care of the new traitor himself. It was just what he needed to brighten his day.

CHAPTER THIRTEEN

Koby jumped up and grabbed the top of the stone fence. He pulled himself up and peeked into the small field. Zolo was still tied to the post. He was completely alone. Seeing that the coast was clear, Koby scuttled up the wall and climbed over. He didn't like doing this. But it was the only way to help his new friend. He ran up to Zolo and began untying the ropes.

Zolo opened his eyes and raised his head. "What are you doing, small fry?" he asked. "Do you want the entire navy coming after you?"

"It's funny, I always wanted to join the navy," said Koby. "But not a navy like this one." He had trouble pulling apart the tight knots.

"Small fry, I can't escape," Zolo explained. "I made a deal. One month."

"But they're going to execute you tomorrow!" Koby replied.

"They're what?" asked Zolo.

"Captain Morgan's son is not going to keep his part of the deal," Koby explained. "He's going to execute you."

"That bilge rat!" growled Zolo.

Koby tried a different knot. The first one was tied too tightly. "You should have seen how mad Luffy became when he found out," said Koby. "And now they're after him."

The boy moved to a third knot. He wished that he'd brought a knife. The knots were too hard to untie. "Look, Mr. Zolo, I'm not asking you to become a pirate. I'm just asking you to help this one pirate this one time!" Koby tried to hurry, but he was getting nowhere. "Luffy saved me. And the way I see it, you're the only one who can save him. And he's the only one who can save you. So it's really an even trade."

Suddenly, the metal gates swung open. "You have been caught red-handed committing an act of treason," boomed a loud voice.

Koby began to shiver. A giant man with a huge battle axe stepped into the yard. He was followed by ten armed sailors. As the group approached, Koby saw that the battle axe was attached to the man's arm in place of his right hand. It had to be Captain "Axe-Hand" Morgan.

The captain halted his men twenty yards away. "Now prepare to face the firing squad!" he said.

The sailors raised their rifles and aimed them at Koby and Zolo. Koby trembled as he stared down the barrels of the rifles.

CHAPTER FOURTEEN

Across the island, Luffy knew he'd have to think quickly to get Zolo's sword back. He faced down the soldiers and laughed, pulling Helmeppo in front of him. "You wouldn't chance hitting the captain's son, would you?"

The men glanced at each other, unsure of what to do. That was the chance Luffy needed. With Helmeppo in front of him, he charged toward them. Luffy and his prisoner smashed into the four sailors sending them flying against the corridor walls.

Luffy continued until Helmeppo raised a finger. "Here," he said, pointing to a closed door.

Luffy kicked in the door and marched inside. He dragged Morgan's son behind him. Helmeppo's room was decorated as extravagantly as the man dressed. Fine paintings lined the walls and antique furniture was sprinkled throughout.

However, it didn't take long to spot what he was looking for. Three samurai swords were propped up in a corner. Luffy let go of Morgan's son and ran over to them. He snatched them up and spun back to Helmeppo. "Which one of these swords belongs to Zolo?" he asked.

Seeing the swords, Helmeppo's eyes rolled and he crumpled to the floor, unconscious.

Luffy couldn't decide between the swords so he kept all three. He strapped them to his back and was about to leave when something caught his eye. From Helmeppo's window, he could see the large field below. It made sense since the captain's son would take great pleasure from watching Zolo tied up every day. But what Luffy saw gave him no pleasure whatsoever. He saw Zolo, Koby, and Captain

Morgan and his men. The sailors had rifles aimed at the pirate hunter and were about to fire.

Luffy had to do something. He opened the window and grabbed both sides of the window frame. He slowly stepped backward, his arms stretching longer and longer.

CHAPTER FIFTEEN

Koby covered his eyes. He couldn't bear to watch. Usually, prisoners were given blindfolds at firing squads. Now he knew why.

Captain Morgan laughed from across the field. "Since we were almost on the same side, Zolo, united in our fight to rid this world of pirate scum, I'll grant you one final wish."

"We could never be on the same side," said Zolo. "But here's my final wish. Take that oversized axe on the end of your arm and chop that head-shaped barnacle off the top of your neck!"

Morgan roared with laughter. "Let's see how funny you are after I've riddled you with more holes than a fishing net!" He raised his axe into the air. "Sailors, ready . . . aim . . ."

"Gum Gum Rocket!" said a distant voice.

Koby looked up to see Luffy soaring toward them. He flew from the tower and landed gracefully onto the field. The boy stood proudly between Koby and the firing squad. "Luffy, no!" shouted Koby.

"Fire!" roared Morgan.

The sailors fired their rifles. Each and every shot struck Luffy in the chest. However, the bullets pushed through his rubber body, stretching to the other side. Long tendrils of skin stretched like rubber bands. Then Luffy's body snapped back and the bullets sailed toward the sailors. The men had to duck as their own bullets fired back at them.

"What?!" asked Zolo.

Luffy laughed and pointed at Captain Morgan. "Looks like your little plan backfired. But mine is right on course!"

"Who is that straw hat?" asked Morgan.

"I'm Monkey D. Luffy!" said Luffy. "And I'm going to be King of the Pirates!"

Koby shook his head. Here he goes again.

CHAPTER SIXTEEN

Luffy ran to Zolo and held out the swords. "I couldn't figure out which one was yours, so I brought all three."

Zolo smiled. "I practice *Santoryu*, so I use three swords. They're *all* mine."

Luffy looked at the swords. "You know, if you fight the navy with me now, you'll become an outlaw and always be on the run. So what's it going to be? Stay tied up or help me fight these sailors?"

"If my choice is between becoming a pirate,

and staying here, with no hope of a future," said Zolo. "Then I've made my decision. You've got yourself a pirate!"

Luffy was thrilled. "For real? You're going to join my pirate crew?"

"No deal unless you untie me," Zolo replied. "And I'm talking right now!"

Captain Morgan howled in frustration. "Those who defy us will feel the blades of our cutlasses," he bellowed. "Show them no mercy!"

The sailors set down their rifles and hesitantly drew their swords. They slowly moved in.

Luffy got to work on Zolo's bonds. They were tied very tightly.

"Hurry up," said Koby. "Morgan's men are going to get us!"

"Haven't you ever untied a knot?" asked Zolo.

"I'm trying," said Luffy. "The knot's too tight. It won't budge."

The sailors moved in faster. They seemed to sense the helplessness of their prey.

"We don't have all day," Zolo growled. "Come on!"

Luffy tugged on another part of the rope. "Uh-oh. I think I made it tighter by mistake."

The sailors broke into a run. They yelled as they approached. They raised their sharp swords over their heads.

Zolo waved an open hand. "Give me my swords, quick!"

Luffy stopped fiddling with the rope and unsheathed one of the swords. He placed it in Zolo's open palm. With amazing speed, the pirate hunter slashed the ropes with the razor sharp blade. Once free, he grabbed the other two swords and leapt toward the group of sailors. In unison, the men brought their swords down upon Zolo. With a sword in each hand, and one held with his mouth, Zolo blocked every attacking blade at once.

"Wow!" shouted Luffy. "How cool was that?"

Zolo held the blades steady, keeping the sailors at bay. "Don't anyone move," he told them through clenched teeth. "Or it'll be your last."

The sailors froze in position. They did exactly

as Zolo instructed. Except for quivering in fear, none of them moved a muscle.

Zolo glanced back at the boys. "Luffy, I told you I would join your pirate crew and I don't intend to go back on my word. But I'm going to make one stipulation that involves something more important to me than anything else in my life. You need to know that like you, I'm also pursuing my dream," said Zolo.

"You are?" asked Luffy.

"Yes," replied Zolo. "I'm going to be the best master swordsman who ever lived! If being part of your crew ever gets in the way of fulfilling my dream, you'll regret it."

"I expect nothing less than the best," said Luffy. "In fact, you'll need to be the best swordsman if you're going to be in my crew!"

Zolo spun around, knocking the sailors backwards. He turned to Luffy. "Big talker. You better be able to deliver because I intend for the world to know my name, even if it is notorious."

"Why are you just standing around?" growled Morgan. "Get them! Now!"

Zolo raised his swords, preparing for another attack.

"Don't worry," said Luffy. "I've got you covered. Now duck!" Zolo did as instructed as Luffy spun in a circle. "Gum Gum Whip!"

In one turn, Luffy stretched out his leg. His long limb reached out and swatted the sailors as if they were pieces on a chess board. They tumbled to the ground.

"Wow!" yelled Koby. "What a move!"

"How did you do that?" asked Zolo.

Luffy laughed. "I ate the Gum Gum fruit and got special powers."

Zolo's eyes widened. "That's a Cursed Fruit!"

"Cursed Fruit?" asked one of the sailors.

"There's no way we can fight a rubber man," said another.

"Am I hearing things?" asked the captain. "What a bunch of cowards!" He stomped forward. "I'm in command here and either you do what I say when I say it or I invite you to shake hands with this." He held out his battle axe.

"Your axe doesn't scare me!" yelled Luffy. "But your face does." He ran full steam ahead toward the evil captain.

"Luffy!" shouted Koby.

Luffy didn't listen. He balled a fist and stretched back his arm. It was time for this captain to get the same treatment as Captain Alvida. As he closed in, he swung his long arm toward the captain's gut. But just as it was about to hit, the captain swung his axe. Luffy's fist merely bounced off of the flat part of the large blade.

"You'll be sorry you did that, Straw Hat!" growled the captain. He ripped away his jacket and tossed it to the ground. "No one messes with Captain 'Axe-Hand' Morgan!"

"Nice to meet you Axe," said Luffy. He leveled his gaze. "I'm Luffy."

Morgan charged him, swinging his giant axe. Luffy flipped backwards, just above the sharp blade. The captain charged again, chopping at Luffy with each step. Luffy easily dodged the massive blows. On the last attack, Luffy sprang into the air, then came down hard at the captain. He slammed the bottom of his wooden sandal into the captain's face. The ugly giant dropped to the ground.

"Captain!" yelled one of the sailors. "Are you okay?"

Morgan stumbled to his feet. "I'm not the one you should worry about." He leveled his axe at Luffy. "He is!"

The captain raised his axe high above his head. As he rushed toward Luffy, the boy sprang forward, spinning toward the villain like a human drill. His head slammed into the captain's steel jaw and sent him flying. Morgan tumbled across the dusty field.

Luffy wasn't finished. He hopped onto the captain's chest and began pounding him. "Now you listen to me," he shouted between punches. "You and your navy . . ." He punched him some more. ". . . are ruining Koby's lifelong dream!"

"Stop it!" yelled a familiar voice. "That punching bag is my father!"

Luffy looked up to see Helmeppo holding a large war hammer over Koby's head. The captain's son must have snuck onto the field during the battle.

Fury flashed in Helmeppo's eyes. "One more punch and you can say good-bye to your friend!" Helmeppo pulled Koby close. "I'll pummel his head flatter than the shape of the Earth."

CHAPTER SEVENTEEN

Koby shook as Helmeppo's grip tightened. He looked up at the large war hammer poised above his head. From what he knew of Helmeppo, he knew the man was crazy enough to follow through with his threats.

"One more move out of you, rubber boy, and four eyes gets it!" shouted Helmeppo. "We run this town and we're going to run you out!"

Koby was tired of being scared. He was tired of other people fighting his battles for him. What's more, he was tired of people like Captain Morgan and his son ruining the good name of the navy.

"Don't give in!" Koby yelled. "You've got to stand up to them and not worry about me. They can't win!"

"Shut up," yelled Helmeppo.

Luffy put his hands on his hips and laughed. "You're a good guy, Koby." He held up a fist. "Let me explain things to Helmeppo, up close and personal."

Koby could feel the man quiver as Luffy stepped forward. "Don't you move!" ordered Helmeppo. "You better not think I'm bluffing. I'll hammer him!"

Just then, Morgan shook his head. The hulking captain stumbled to his feet and raised his axe behind Luffy.

"Watch out!" shouted Koby.

Luffy either didn't hear Koby's warning or didn't care. He pulled back his fist, and stretched out his arm. "Gum Gum . . ."

"Don't you realize who I am, rubber boy?" boomed Morgan. He raised his axe higher.

"Father! Would you hurry up already!" shouted Helmeppo.

"Gum Gum Blast!" shouted Luffy.

Just then, Koby saw an amazing display of pirate teamwork. Luffy's arm rocketed toward Helmeppo just as Morgan's axe sliced toward Luffy's head. The rubber boy's attack connected. He struck Helmeppo in the face and knocked him down the field. Captain Morgan wasn't so lucky. Just as he was about to chop Luffy to pieces, Zolo leaped toward him and blocked his axe with one of his swords. Then the former pirate hunter spun around and kicked the captain in the face. Morgan flew backwards and landed in the dirt. He was out cold.

Luffy didn't even look back. "Good job, Zolo!"

Zolo smiled. "The feeling's mutual, Captain."

"Captain Morgan has been defeated," said one of the sailors.

"I don't believe it," said another.

Luffy and Zolo stood back-to-back, ready for the next attack. "If there's anyone who still wants to capture us, please step forward," said Zolo.

Then, to Koby's surprise and delight, the sailors

cheered. They removed their caps and threw them into the air. "We're free!" they cried. "Woo-hoo!"

"What's this?" asked Luffy. "Celebrating their captain's defeat? How strange."

Koby ran up to Luffy and Zolo. "They hated him and they were too scared to admit it!"

Just then, Zolo swayed and collapsed.

"Is he wounded?" asked Koby.

"My stomach..." mumbled Zolo. "I need food."

CHAPTER EIGHTEEN

Back at the restaurant, Luffy shoveled food into his mouth. It was a good thing his stomach was made of rubber like the rest of him. He was going to need it.

Zolo pushed back from the table. "Eight helpings is my limit." His bandana was tied around his arm, revealing his short green hair. "I went three whole weeks without food, but now I'm full."

"That's all you can eat?" asked Luffy. "Eight helpings?"

"I hope you're not claiming to have a bigger appetite than me," said Zolo.

Luffy cleaned his plate. "This serving makes ten. Isn't that right Koby?"

Koby waved his hands. "No way, Luffy. Don't get me involved."

"Eat all you want," said Rika's mother. "You two saved our town and my girl. It's the least we can do."

Smiling, Rika sat across from Luffy. "You were so brave to fight Captain Morgan."

"You haven't seen anything yet," announced Luffy. "Now that I have a crew, it's only a matter of time before our adventures begin and I become King of the Pirates!"

"Hey, who else is in the crew besides us, Luffy?" asked Zolo.

Luffy cocked his head. "Huh?"

"Well, it's about time I found out who my fellow pirates are going to be," Zolo replied. He wiped his mouth with a napkin. "You know, the quartermaster, gunner, surgeon, head cook. How big a crew do we have?"

Luffy grinned. "Just you so far."

Zolo nearly fell out of his seat. "Just . . ."

"Yup! Me and you! Just us two," said Luffy.

Zolo crossed his arms. "A crew is usually more than two people, you know."

"Yeah, well, I believe in running a tight ship," said Luffy. He stood and looked out the window. He saw his small boat bobbing up and down at the docks. "By the way, you can see our ship from here."

Zolo joined him at the window. "That?!" He pointed to Luffy's boat. "Are you kidding? I've been in life rafts bigger than that thing." He plopped back in his chair and sighed. "Well, I guess a deal's a deal."

"We'll have a really big ship in no time at all. You'll see!" said Luffy. "We're going to have the coolest pirate ship in the whole wide world!"

Luffy could picture the vessel in his mind. It was a huge pirate ship with three masts loaded with sails. He even had the design picked out for his pirate flag. It would be a skull and crossed bones like other pirates. But his skull would wear a straw hat, just like his own. He'd even paint the symbol on the ship's main sail.

Zolo shook his head. "It's my own fault. I should never have joined his crew without checking his references first."

Koby giggled. "Luffy's great with the big picture but I don't think he works out the details in advance."

Luffy slapped Zolo on the back. "Don't worry, we'll have a great team."

"Where are you going to go on your first pirate adventure?" asked Rika.

Luffy spread his arms wide. "We're going to the Grand Line. To find Gold Roger's treasure!"

"Just the two of you, at the Grand Line?" asked Koby. "It's too dangerous!"

"What's the Grand Line?" asked Rika.

"Between the great two oceans of the world lies a huge continent called the Red Line," explained Koby. "At the center of this continent is a town and the Grand Line runs at right angles around it."

"It's where the legendary King of Pirates, Gold

Roger, hid his fortune," Luffy added. "It's a treasure called One Piece. It's more valuable than all the treasures in all the world. Pirates from all over are looking for it."

Zolo chimed in. "Yeah, but these days, the Grand Line is a never-ending battlefield at sea. They call it the Cemetery of Pirates."

Rika's mother leaned forward. "Luffy, you do realize that according to legend, once someone enters the Grand Line, they never return."

"Is that so?" asked Luffy. "Well, we're going to the Grand Line and that's that."

Zolo laughed. "It doesn't scare me one bit."

"But you should be scared!" said Koby.

"It'll be fun," said Zolo. "You should join us."

Koby hung his head. "Even though I'll miss you both, my dream has been to join the navy." He looked up at Luffy. "But what do you think, Luffy, can we still stay friends?"

"Sure thing," Luffy replied. "We're going our separate ways but we'll always be friends."

"You know, Koby, I don't want to burst your bubble," said Zolo. "But you've been sailing with pirates for two years. If the navy found out they'd never enlist you. They might even put you under arrest."

Koby frowned. "Yeah, I thought of that."

"Excuse us!" said a deep voice at the door. Luffy turned to see a naval commander flanked by six other sailors. He pointed to Luffy. "Is it true that you call yourself a pirate?"

"Sure do," replied Luffy. "And not just any pirate. I'm on my way to become King of the Pirates."

The commander tugged nervously at his collar. "We're grateful that you helped us get rid of Captain Morgan. Now we can restore peace and honor to our base. But as naval officers, we won't harbor outlaws any longer."

CHAPTER NINETEEN

Koby wasn't so surprised by what the commander said. Even though Luffy was his friend, naval officers hunted pirates. That's just the way it was.

"Our job is to uphold the law, and pirates abide by no law but their own," said the commander. "We promise not to pursue you but you must leave this island at once."

A small crowd formed outside of the restaurant. The townspeople were shocked by what they heard.

"Who are you guys kidding?!" asked one woman.

"They saved our lives!" shouted an older man.

"These guys are heroes!" said another.

The entire mob shouted insults at the commander and his men. However, the sailors didn't budge.

Luffy stood and straitened his hat. "I guess we'll go." He waved at Rika and her mother. "Thanks so much for the delicious supper!"

Rika ran up and hugged him. "Please don't go," she pleaded. "I'm going to miss you."

Luffy patted her on the head. "You heard what the man said." He walked toward the door. Zolo grabbed his swords and followed.

Koby waved good-bye. He was going to miss Luffy but he knew this was the way it had to be.

The commander pointed to Koby. "You're also a part of their crew, aren't you?"

Koby's jaw dropped "I . . . uh . . ."

"I can't hear you!" the commander shouted.

"Well . . ." said Koby. "You see . . ."

The naval officer spun around and grabbed Luffy's shoulder. "Hold on! Isn't he with you?"

"With us?" asked Luffy. He looked at Koby and grinned. "Well, let me tell you how it all began."

Koby couldn't believe it. "Luffy! Don't tell them!"

"So, there's this pirate named Alvida or something." Luffy puffed out his cheeks. "She's as big as a killer whale!"

"No!" shouted Koby. He grew furious. They would never let him join the navy if they thought he was a pirate like Luffy.

Luffy strolled over to Koby. "She would swing an iron club around and look so mean. This guy was at her beck and call for two whole years." He leaned over and poked Koby on the side of the head. "Isn't that right, Koby? You worked for Captain Alvida."

Koby felt himself tremble again. But this time, he trembled with anger. "Luffy, don't," he said between clenched teeth. "I told you this was my dream!" Luffy poked him again and that was all Koby could take. He balled up a fist and smashed Luffy in the face.

"Hit a pirate will you?" asked Luffy. He leaped onto Koby. The two traded punches as they scuffled around the room.

"Stop it right now!" ordered the commander.

Zolo moved in and pulled Luffy off. "Enough!" he shouted. "You made your point."

The commander stepped closer. "Then I was wrong after all. You two are enemies." He pointed to Koby. "That means you can stay." He turned to Luffy and Zolo. "But you two must go."

Zolo released Luffy. The boy straightened his vest and smiled at Koby. Then he and Zolo marched out of the restaurant.

Koby slowly got to his feet. He finally got it. Luffy had done it on purpose. He picked a fight so Koby could stay. He was a true friend to the end.

As the naval officer turned to watch them leave, Koby planted his feet behind him. "Commander!" The boy stood at attention. "Please, Commander, let me enlist in the navy. I promise to serve with unwavering strength and courage."

The man turned and peered into Koby's eyes.

One of his men leaned in as well. "Commander! I am opposed to this suggestion," said the sailor. "He has spent too much time with pirates. He could be a spy."

Koby looked the man straight in the eyes. "I'm going to be a naval officer and serve with integrity!"

The commander placed his hands behind his back and slowly paced around Koby. "Joining the navy is no easy task," he said. "Your life will be filled with danger." He stopped in front of him and leaned in. "Can you handle it?"

"Yes . . ." said Koby.

"Can you handle it, sailor?" he shouted.

Koby's heart soared. He called him *sailor*! That meant he was going to let Koby join the navy.

Koby held his head high and gave a salute. "Yes, sir!"

CHAPTER TWENTY

Luffy inhaled the sweet salty air as they neared the docks. He couldn't wait to get back to sea and back on his quest. He could almost smell the adventure in the air.

"You were such a bad actor back there," said Zolo. "I wouldn't quit your day job if I were you."

Luffy chuckled. "I wanted to help Koby, but now he's on his own."

"It's a good time to go," said Zolo, looking around. "Thanks to your performance, everybody hates us now. But I guess that's how pirates should always leave a town. Don't you agree?"

Luffy laughed. "Yeah, I sure do." He untied his boat's mooring line as Zolo climbed aboard. Luffy tossed him the rope and climbed in as well. He unfurled the sail and the wind began to push them out to sea.

"Luffy!" yelled Koby.

Luffy turned to see Koby running down after them. The young boy stopped at the bottom of the steps and stood at attention.

"Thank you, Pirate Luffy!" Koby shouted. "Sailor Koby is forever at your service."

"Let's see, a navy guy thanking the pirate who beat him up," said Zolo. "That has to be a first."

Koby took off his hat and waved as their boat pulled away from shore. "Lots of luck, Koby! Good-bye!"

Koby was soon joined by the commander and the rest of his sailors. The commander stood at attention. Koby and the rest of his men did the same. "Sailors, salute!" ordered the commander. Every one of them gave a crisp salute.

Luffy waved harder. "See you!"

As their boat sailed out of the harbor, Luffy heard the commander barking orders at his men. "Saluting a pirate ship is a direct violation of navy protocol. I am therefore revoking all meal privileges for one day. Understand?!"

"Yes, sir!" answered the sailors in unison.

Luffy watched the island grow smaller and smaller. He knew Koby was going to be just fine. And even though Koby was in the navy and Luffy was a pirate, he knew they would always be friends.

As Zolo steered their boat toward the open sea, Luffy took his favorite spot on the ship's bow. He smiled as they sailed away from the setting sun. "Was there ever a finer pirate crew than us, Zolo?" he asked.

"I'm sure some great adventures await us, Luffy," said Zolo.

"You're right about that!" Luffy laughed and turned his face into the wind. "And I'm going to be King of the Pirates!"